3/11

For Tom.
And Rick, in absentia.
~ J.L.C.

For Peter, who leaves me
alone but is always there.
~ L.C.

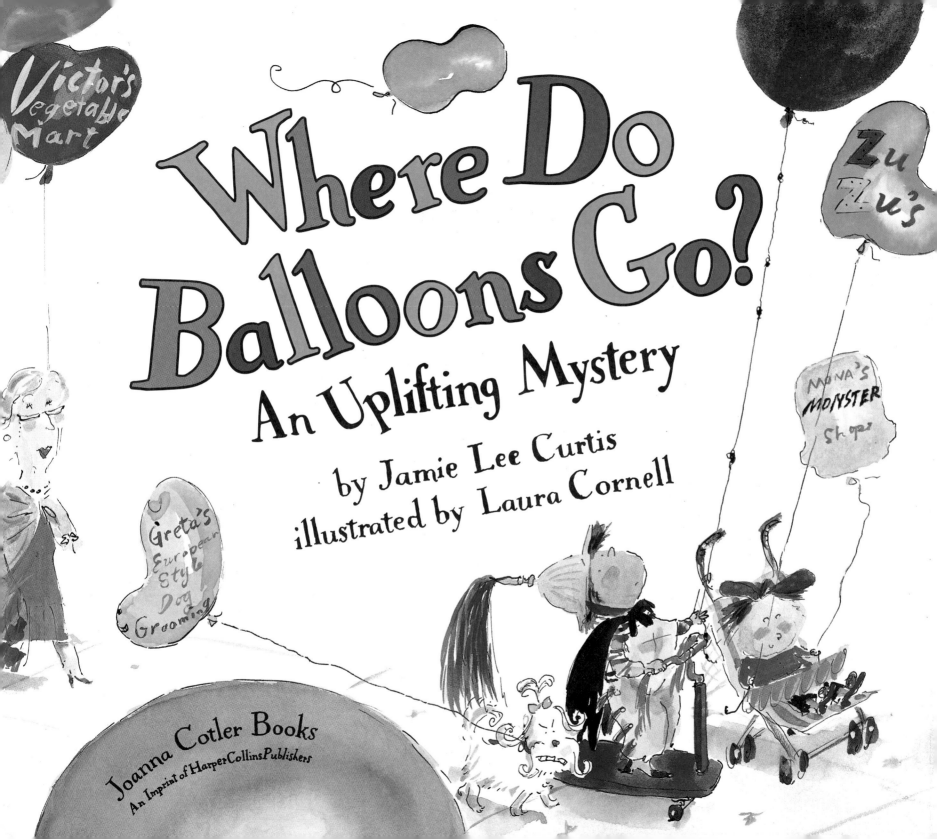

Where do balloons go
when you let them go free?
It can happen by accident.

Where do they go
when they float far away?

Do they ever catch cold
and need somewhere to stay?

Do they keep going up?
Can they ever just stop?
I'm sure that they're always
concerned that they'll POP—
maybe caught up in wires
pushed by the breeze
poked by tall buildings
or tangled in trees?

Are they always alone?
Do they meet up in pairs?

Do they ever get married and make balloon heirs?

Do they ever write postcards, e-mail or fax?

Forty-fifth Annual Rubber Convention, Airville, home of famous Hot Air Springs and the wading pool.

Dear Zu Zu,
   Enjoying the rubber samples and hot air treatments. Keeping full and shiny.
      Wish you were here. See you soon on Main Street.

AIR MAIL
(ha!)

Miss ZuZu Zapateria
1200 Main Street
USA

Do they ever just let down their strings and relax?

Maybe they're better away from the smog

being twisted by clowns

or chased by my dog.

But floating so high
without worries or cares
don't they miss birthdays,
parties and fairs?

Where do balloons go?
What's really up there?
As far as I see,
it's just sky and air.

Can plain balloons read
balloons printed with words?

If one's loose in Norway
and one in Tibet
and one in Alaska
and Mass-a-chu-SETTS

do they all meet up high

TOM'S
CANINE
T...

Greta's
European
Style
Dog
Grooming

A BIG

and one in Bolivia,
England and France

Do some go so far
that they end up in space?
Do they challenge the rockets
to float them a race?

And what if the leader
gets close to the sun?
We know rubber melts.
That wouldn't be fun.

Then does it get quiet?
Do the stars give a shove?
And send it on high
to that place up above?

Does it float there forever
remembering me?
And know that I'm happy
that it's floating free?

Where _do_ balloons go?
It's a mystery, I know.
So just hold on tight
till you have to

let go.

Thanks to Jamie and
Joanna for sending me
soaring. To Lilly, my
constant subject.
~L.C.

Thanks to Joanna, Phyllis and
Laura for inflating it. And
to Rachel Evans for asking
the question.
~J.L.C.